Dawn
Diary Two

Other books by
Ann M. Martin

P.S. Longer Letter Later
(written with Paula Danziger)
Leo the Magnificat
Rachel Parker, Kindergarten Show-off
Eleven Kids, One Summer
Ma and Pa Dracula
Yours Turly, Shirley
Ten Kids, No Pets
Slam Book
Just a Summer Romance
Missing Since Monday
With You and Without You
Me and Katie (the Pest)
Stage Fright
Inside Out
Bummer Summer

THE KIDS IN MS. COLMAN'S CLASS series
BABY-SITTERS LITTLE SISTER series
THE BABY-SITTERS CLUB mysteries
THE BABY-SITTERS CLUB series
CALIFORNIA DIARIES series

California Diaries #7

Dawn

Diary Two

Ann M. Martin

SCHOLASTIC INC.
New York Toronto London Auckland Sydney

ISBN 0-590-01846-9

10 9 8 7 6 5 4 3 2 1   7 8 9/9 0 1/0

Printed in the U.S.A   40

First Scholastic printing, June 1998

*The author gratefully acknowledges
Jeanne Betancourt
for her help in
preparing this manuscript.*

Journals are for talking about your feelings. Here's what I am feeling:

Lonely.

Tense.

Sad.

I look at what I've just written and I am amazed. None of it sounds like me. I used to be an upbeat kind of person. I tried not to show my negative feelings to the rest of the world. But I can't deny that I feel them. This is me, Dawn Schafer, right now.

Lonely.

Tense.

Sad.

I know why I'm upset. Sunny, my very best friend in the whole world, has turned into an entirely different person.

Make that my _former_ best friend.

The only other time I have felt this terrible was when Mom and Dad were first divorced. And I had to leave California to live on the other side of the country with Mom. I hated leaving Sunny. And I missed her the whole time I lived on the East Coast.

Sunny was one of the main reasons I moved back to California. When her mother was diagnosed with lung cancer I _thought_ Sunny would need her best friend close by. I'm glad I'm here for Mrs. Winslow, but I was _totally_ wrong about what Sunny needed.

It's so ironic. I moved back to be close to Sunny and we aren't even speaking to each other.

Maybe Sunny and I were only best friends because we were neighbors. No, that doesn't make sense. We used to do absolutely everything together. We could finish each other's sentences. The phone would ring, and I would know it was Sunny before I picked up the receiver. I could walk into her house anytime and feel like a member of the family. Sunny could do that at our house too. Even after Dad remarried and Carol moved in with us. Another irony — Sunny gets along better with Carol than I do.

I hate that Sunny isn't acting like Sunny anymore. She's changed from this clever, considerate, always-there-for-you friend into a sneaky, inconsiderate, never-to-be-trusted-again stranger. Sunny is the last person I would have expected to change like that. Especially now, when her family is going through such a hard time. I mean, we have to face it — Mrs. Winslow is . . . Well, they don't have much hope anymore that she will ever get better. Just writing that made me cry. Mrs. Winslow is wonderful, like a second mother to me. I'm a lot closer to her than I'll ever be to Carol.

What I don't understand is why Sunny is turning into some other person just when her mother and father need her the most. It's like she doesn't care about anyone but herself. She skips school, hangs out with older guys, is dressing in a different way that's very . . . <u>adult.</u> It's like she doesn't care what people think about her. But what bothers me the most is that <u>Sunny is not there for her mother.</u>

Instead of visiting her mother in the hospital, she's been over at our place an awful lot, taking care of Carol because she's having a baby. I do feel sorry for Carol. The doctor ordered her to stay in bed for the last three months of her pregnancy. She can't even get up to go to the bathroom. We have to bring her a bedpan. I know it's hard on Carol, but it's also a lot of extra work for Dad and me. Even Jeff is pitching in. But we didn't expect Sunny to help out. Especially not when it meant neglecting her own sick mother. If my mother were sick I would be with her as much as possible. But I don't want to think about that possibility. It's too awful.

An ambulance just drove up our street and pulled into the Winslows' driveway. Mrs. Winslow has been getting sicker every day. So she's either going back to the hospital or . . . I want to run over there to find out what's going on. I want to help. But how can I when Sunny and I aren't even talking? I'm so worried about Mrs. Winslow.

Carol just rang the little bell she uses to say she needs something. Later . . .

Mrs. Winslow has gone back to the hospital. Carol and I saw them take her out on a stretcher. Mr. Winslow was walking beside his wife. He didn't go in the ambulance but followed it in his car. He looked really sad. He had been so happy that his wife was home again. We all were. We hoped she'd be able to stay this time.

At first I thought Sunny wasn't home and that's why she wasn't with her mother. But then I spotted her peeking out from behind the blinds in the living room. I told Carol that if it were my mother I'd be in the ambulance with her. Carol said that might not be what Mrs. Winslow wanted.

"Why wouldn't she?" I asked. "Sunny is her daughter."

"Maybe she's going later." Carol patted her big belly. "I can't help remembering that my baby and I were almost taken away in an ambulance."

"Thanks to Sunny," I pointed out.

"Accidents happen," said Carol.

She has been standing up for Sunny a lot lately. What almost happened to Carol and the baby wasn't an _accident_. It was Sunny's fault. Plain and simple.

I know it was almost two months ago, but I can't stop thinking about it. Sunny _promised_ she'd watch out for Carol, who was not supposed to get out of bed under any circumstances. Sunny _promised_ Mrs. Bruen that she'd keep an eye on the pot of stew that was cooking on the stove. And what did Sunny do when a cute guy came driving up our block, blowing his horn? _She ran out of the house_, leaving the stew on the stove and Carol helpless in bed.

So what happened? My former best friend, Sunshine Winslow, almost burned our house down and put the lives of _two_ people in grave danger.

And what did Sunny do about it?

Did she apologize?

Did she act like she cared?

No. _She ran away_. And when she finally came back, she had an attitude and made all sorts of excuses for herself. She just hung around waiting for everyone to say it was okay. Well, it _wasn't_ okay. _It isn't_ okay. We don't need someone like that around here.

I can't stop thinking about the fight Sunny and I had that night. I play it over and over in my head like a movie.

I came home from shopping. The house smelled smoky. Mrs. Bruen told me what had happened and that Sunny had run out. Mrs. Bruen, who is usually so sweet-tempered and understanding, was furious with Sunny. Everybody was. I figured Sunny wouldn't come back and she certainly wouldn't continue sleeping over at our house, in _my room._ So I took some plastic garbage bags to my room and put all of Sunny's stuff in them and folded up her cot. Then I sat down at my desk to do my homework.

After awhile I thought I heard Sunny's voice in the house. At first I ignored it. Then I started worrying about Carol. I didn't want Sunny to upset her. So I went to Dad and Carol's room. I couldn't believe what I saw. Dad, Carol, and Mrs. Bruen were sitting around with Sunny having a friendly talk. I turned and went back to my room without saying anything. Nobody seemed to notice. I figured they were all forgiving Sunny and then she'd leave.

About an hour later I heard a gentle tap on my door. I thought it was Dad saying good night. But Sunny walked in.

"Hi," she said, _like nothing had happened!_

"You're still here," I said. "You're staying?"

"Yeah. Carol and your dad want me to." She put her hands on her hips. "What'd you do with all my stuff?"

"I figured you were going to do what you're always doing these days," I told her.

"And what's that?"

"Run away."

I reminded her that she's been running away a lot lately, ducking out, avoiding anything unpleasant. I tried to help her face the fact that she's letting down her mother, her father, her friends, and herself.

But did that get me anywhere with her?

We ended up yelling at each other. She had the nerve to accuse me of not caring about my stepmother. Who is she to talk to me about how to take care of a parent? I

reminded her that I visit her mother more
than she does.

Her answer to that? "I visit her more
than you know."

"I know all the times you visit her,"
I replied, "because you complain about
every last one." Then Sunny said at least
I had a mom, that I had two of them.

I reminded her that she has a mother
too. Maybe it's time for her to appreciate the
mother she has.

Sunny didn't say anything for a few
seconds. I hoped she was finally seeing how
terrible she'd been acting lately. I hoped we
could start from there and make up.
Instead, she turned and ran out of my
room and the house.

Yes, Sunny running away again.

I couldn't sleep that night. I wanted to
talk over what was happening between
Sunny and me. I still wanted to help her.

I called her house the next day and left
a message on the answering machine.
Around dinnertime I saw her go into her
house. But she didn't call me. I kept
thinking:

Her mother is very sick.

I don't know how awful Sunny must feel.

She needs her friends.

I should be patient, understanding, and forgiving.

I left her another message: "Sunny, it's Dawn, please call me."

She didn't.

I told Maggie about what happened, but she acted like it was just one of those fights friends get into. "It'll pass," she said.

"Maggie, please tell her I want to talk to her," I pleaded.

I still can't believe what Sunny said when Maggie told her I wanted to talk. "If Dawn wants to be friends, all it takes is an apology, a large diamond necklace, a new navel ring, and three years of personal servitude." Like it's a big joke. Ha-ha! Seven years of friendship ending in a lame joke.

Meanwhile, I just heard loud punk music from a car radio outside. I can see an old yellow convertible driving up our block. I think I recognize the guy who's

driving and the couple in the backseat.
They're upperclassmen from Vista.

The driver is honking his horn.

Now Sunny is coming out on
Rollerblades. She's wearing tight short
shorts and a halter top that shows her
navel ring. She's _laughing_ and waving.

The girl and two guys are shouting hi
to her. They think it's really cool that she
already has on her blades.

Sunny climbs into the car without opening
the door. Then she gives the driver a big
kiss and he peels away from the curb.

This is what my _former_ best friend is
doing less than half an hour after her
terminally ill mother went to the hospital in
an ambulance.

I hate being so angry at Sunny. I hate
it.

But really, it's all her fault.

Saturday noon 6/6
Maggie phoned. I've known her even
longer than I've known Sunny, but somehow

we're just not as close. It used to be so much fun when the four of us hung out together. Sunny, Maggie, Jill, and me.

But Jill's been out of the picture so long that I can barely remember what the picture used to look like. She's so childish. I still can't believe that she gave away the secret of Carol's pregnancy. She just blurted it out like a little kid. I'm still mad about that. But really, it goes even deeper. I see Jill in the halls and we just don't _connect_. She's off in her own little world, and I'm stuck here in the real world.

I'm going to the beach tomorrow with Maggie, Amalia (who's really more Maggie's friend than mine), and some of _their_ friends from their band.

I love the beach.

I love to surf.

It'll be a great change of scene.

Who knows? Maybe Maggie and I will become closer. It's worth a try.

There's Carol's bell again. I told her I'd make her a snack and give her a back rub. It must be awful to not be able to get out of bed. The baby will be her reward. I can't help but wonder: what will Mrs. Winslow's reward be?

Sunday afternoon 6/7

Here I am at the beach. I'm writing this on a big rock that juts out into the ocean. I love it here, even when I'm upset. As the waves crash on the sand and retreat, I try to visualize them taking away my bad thoughts and cleansing my spirit.

Maggie and Amalia are sitting on the beach with Rico, Patti, and Bruce. Rico is strumming a guitar. Patti and Bruce are softly tapping out a beat on the cooler. Maggie is singing. She has a beautiful voice and writes the best lyrics. It's cool that she's started to share them with us.

I'm glad I came to the beach today, but I might as well have come alone. I don't feel like part of this crowd.

Earlier, I asked Maggie to go for a walk with me on the beach. She said yes.

But I saw her look back at the others as she stood up, like she really didn't want to leave.

I told Maggie she didn't have to come if she didn't want to. Maggie insisted she wanted to walk with me. She picked up her towel and wrapped it around her waist. "I have to cover up my flab," she whispered.

Flab? Excuse me, but what is she talking about? Maggie is slender with a capital S.

So, as we started our walk, I told her she didn't have any flab. She argued with me about it. That conversation ended with my saying, "Whatever." Then I asked if she'd talked to Sunny lately.

"Not really," she answered. "Friendships change. It happens."

I didn't agree. I wanted to say that the friendship I had with Sunny was deeper than with anyone else in our group. But I realized that might make Maggie feel a little weird, since she was one of our group too.

"Listen," Maggie said, "Rico's playing his guitar. Let's go back."

End of conversation.

I sat on the edge of the blanket and listened to them play for awhile, but I just felt more and more alone. So I went for a long swim and now I'm writing this.

I hope Maggie and her new friends don't want to stay at the beach too late — I promised Dad I'd help make dinner tonight.

Sunday night 6/7

Dad made pasta primavera for dinner, and I made a salad and baked some oatmeal-raisin cookies. I can't talk to him about Sunny. I can't talk to him about much of anything these days, unless it has to do with Carol and the baby.

He'll ask me the usual parent questions like: "How's school?" "Where are you going tonight?" "Did you have a good time at the beach?" "How high were the waves?"

But I don't think he's really listening when I answer. I know he's always thinking about Carol and the baby. Which is only natural. Carol and the baby are his new family. Jeff and I are his old family. And his new family is what's most important to him right now. (Anyway, that's how it feels sometimes.)

We took trays to the bedroom so we could eat with Carol. She sits up in her bed and we sit around her. Carol's big belly is like a centerpiece. The baby is due any day now. Dad oohs and ahhs and is always putting his hand on Carol's stomach to feel the baby. Jeff is fascinated. He loves to watch the baby move. He calls it "The Pod," like it's a character in a sci-fi movie.

Jeff is pretty excited about having a half brother or sister. He seems to genuinely like Carol too. Maybe that's because Jeff is still a child and Carol can act pretty juvenile herself. That sounds mean, but it's true. I guess Carol is basically an okay person. I might even like her if she were someone else's stepmother. But she's my stepmother. Besides, I already have a mother.

Sometimes I feel guilty about not being excited about the baby. I try to show a little enthusiasm, but with all the other things I have on my mind it's not easy. And I don't want to fake it. I hate when people pretend they're happy about something and you can tell they really aren't.

If I felt closer to Carol maybe I'd be more excited about her baby. Maybe not. I mean, it'll only be my half brother or sister. I'll barely get to know it. By the time it's five years old I'll be in college and then I'll probably never live at home again.

Carol wanted to know about the beach and who was there. She misses the ocean and can't wait to get back to surfing. She patted her belly. "We'll be surfing before you know it, Emerson."

"Emerson!" my father said in alarm. "Now, that's a new one."

Carol giggled and said she was just trying a new name on us. Then Dad, Carol, and Jeff were off, talking about their favorite subject — what to name the baby.

Carol suggested we start with the A's and say every name that we liked. Jeff said we should do boys' names first. He's convinced Carol is going to have a boy. She wanted me to be the secretary for this session of the Name Game, but I gave the honor to Jeff. I said I'd clear the dishes and get our dessert. I was pretty bored with the Name Game.

Now, here's something that surprises me. Dad and Carol have had plenty of opportunities to find out the sex of this baby. The pregnancy has been difficult, so Carol had a zillion tests. The doctors and nurses know whether it's a girl or a boy. But Carol doesn't want to know.

"I like the suspense," she always says. "It'll be a nice surprise in the delivery room."

I think Dad would like to know whether he's having a son or a daughter, but he's doing whatever Carol wants. The only reason I wish they'd find out is because it would cut the time they spend on the Name Game in half. I don't really care what they name it. It's more their baby than my sister or brother.

So while my father, brother, and Carol played the Name Game, I brought the dishes to the kitchen, loaded the dishwasher, made coffee for my dad and herbal tea for Carol, poured glasses of milk for Jeff and me, laid the cookies on a plate, put everything on a tray, and went back to the bedroom. I could hear Jeff clowning around about the name Attila, and Dad and Carol laughing.

"Jeff," said Carol with a sigh, "I'd be so happy if I had a boy just like you."

Dad grinned.

"Being a prisoner in this bed isn't so terrible with visitors like you guys," added Carol.

Right, I thought, _and servants like me._

While we ate dessert we gave Jeff names to put on the list. I suggested Brad and Bret. We started with the C's. Then Jeff and I did the dishes, and then I went back to my room and closed the door.

I have to admit it's a relief not to be sharing my room with Sunny, her stuff, and her complaints. Sunny was taking up all the air in my room. It's good to be able to close the door and be alone with my own thoughts — even when they aren't happy ones.

I ate lunch with Maggie and Amalia, who are now going over some ideas Amalia has for the band. We had a pop quiz in math this morning. I think I did okay, but Maggie thinks she flunked it.

"I never do well on those kinds of tests," she complained. "If only I'd known we were having a pop quiz I would have spent more time on math last night."

It's so weird the way Maggie worries about schoolwork. I'm sure she didn't fail the test. She _never_ fails. She's aced every test she has ever taken. I reminded her of that, but I don't think it sank in. Maggie will worry about the test until she gets it back with a big, fat, red 100.

Sunny, on the other hand, cut math. And I don't see her in the lunchroom now either. It's the same old story. She's probably playing hooky.

Why is she doing this?

To Do Today:
* Hospital visit with Mrs. Winslow
* Bookstore for Carol

mystery novel — <u>Nightfall</u> by Randal
Pierce / magazines — <u>My Lucky
Stars</u> / <u>New Parent</u> / <u>Vogue</u>
* Serve dinner, do dishes
* Check with Dad about plane
  reservation for flight to Connecticut —
  request vegetarian meal
* Make schedule for exam preps —
  finals in 5 DAYS!
* Hem jean shorts
* Decide on gifts to buy for Mary
  Anne, Mom, and Richard

    I can't believe I'm going back to
Stoneybrook in two weeks. Here I am in my
room, in my house, in my <u>life</u> in California.
I can't imagine myself on the other side of
the country, in a different room, in a
different house, in my <u>other</u> life. I probably
won't mind being in Stoneybrook once I'm
there. But I'm afraid I will mind not
being <u>here</u>. I'm worried about what will
happen to my life here when I'm not a
part of it.
    Will I have a half brother or half
sister? More important, will the delivery go

okay? How will I feel about having a baby brother or sister?

Will Mrs. Winslow be at home or in the hospital when I leave? What will happen to her during the nine weeks I'm in Stoneybrook? (I hate leaving when she's so sick. That bothers me more than anything.)

Will Sunny run away for good? Sometimes I think that she'll cut out and not come back. She must be so upset.

So why won't she let anyone help her?

Monday afternoon 6/8

I walked into Mrs. Winslow's hospital room and found it empty.

I rushed to the nurses' station in a panic.

They told me she was having a treatment and would be back up in a little while. I was terrified that the worst had happened. But it hadn't. Not this time.

I'm now in her room, which is pretty cheerful for a hospital room. A purple-and-orange quilt she made out of her own tie-dyed fabric is at the foot of the bed. A bouquet of roses and a lily plant make the room smell a little better than most hospital rooms. Just a little. Also, on the windowsill are a framed finger painting that Sunny did when she was in kindergarten and a framed photo of Sunny and her dad with their arms around each other.

Ducky gave me a ride to the hospital. He said he was going that way anyway, but I know he just wanted to talk to me about Sunny. Ducky is such a great guy. He's funny, kind, considerate, and cute. It's hard to find all of those qualities in one person, much less a sixteen-year-old guy. He's been a good friend to Sunny. Maybe _too_ good. I think Sunny takes advantage of Ducky and the fact that he has his own car. If she snaps her fingers Ducky is there to drive her wherever she wants to go.

"So," he said as soon as we drove out of the school parking lot, "are you and Sunny still not talking?"

"Nope," I replied.

I didn't tell him _why_ nothing had changed.

I didn't tell him that she went out blading just minutes after her mother returned to the hospital. I figured Sunny should keep whatever friends she can.

"I think Sunny needs you, Dawn," Ducky said.

"_She_ doesn't seem to think so," I told him. "I tried. I really did. I left her messages and she didn't call back. And she's making _jokes_ about our not being friends. It's like she doesn't care about anything she used to care about — me, her parents, school, her reputation, the future."

Ducky sighed and ran his hand through his hair. "I know you tried," he said. "But sometimes you have to stick with your friends even when they aren't so nice to you. They just need you to be around."

"It's hard to be around someone who isn't talking to you and keeps running away," I muttered.

"I know," Ducky said softly.

I realized that Ducky was thinking about Alex. It can't be much fun to be around your oldest friend when he's so depressed — which seems to be most of the time these days. Ducky spends a lot of time with Alex, even when Alex acts like he doesn't want Ducky around. I'm sure Alex's dark moods bring Ducky down. I guess Ducky hopes that simply by being there he's helping Alex, just like he's trying to help Sunny. I thought, <u>That's what I should be doing for Sunny.</u> I silently resolved to try one more time to make up with her.

Ducky opened his door and jumped out. For a minute I thought he was going to visit Mrs. Winslow too. But he'd gotten out of the car to open the door for me.

Ducky is the only guy I know who has manners like that. He should have a more sophisticated name than Ducky. Something like Emerson. Or, Randal the Third. Or maybe Maximillian. If Carol and Dad named their baby Maximillian, they could call him Max. That's a cute nickname. Or Maxine if it's a girl. Max is a great nickname for a girl too.

Monday night 6/8

I can't concentrate on my science homework. I have to review the organs of the human body. The illustration in my biology book is of a healthy body. But all I can think about is Mrs. Winslow's _unhealthy_ body.

Mr. Winslow told my father that the cancer has spread to her bones, so they're trying some new chemotherapy treatment. That's why she's in the hospital this time. When they brought her to the room after the treatment I could see that she was exhausted and in pain.

"I'm sorry you had to come back to the hospital," I said after I kissed her hello.

"Me too," she said weakly. "But I'm still fighting, Dawn."

I squeezed her hand. "I'm glad. I'm really glad."

I pulled a chair up next to the bed.

"So, how are you?" she asked.

I didn't want to tell her how I really was. She had enough problems. So I said, "Okay. Great."

"I know things aren't so great between

you and Sunny these days," she said. "You aren't speaking to one another."

I was surprised that Mrs. Winslow knew. I hoped that Sunny hadn't made a big deal out of it with her parents. They had enough trouble. I wondered what Sunny had said about me.

"We did have an argument," I replied very carefully, "but we'll get over it."

"Do you want to talk about it?" asked Mrs. Winslow.

I wanted to tell my side of the story, but I didn't want her to worry about our problems when she should be putting all of her energy into fighting the cancer.

"It's nothing to worry about," I said. "Really."

Mrs. Winslow put her hand over mine. "Yes," she said softly. "It'll work out. It always does with you two."

I wanted so much to tell her that I didn't think it would "work out" this time, to tell her the whole awful story. I wanted to cry on her shoulder, just the way I did when I skinned my elbow falling off Sunny's trampoline when we were kids. But we weren't kids anymore, and I was there to cheer up Sunny's mother.

"I'm very glad Sunny has you, Dawn," she continued. "I know that no matter what happens she can count on you."

I nodded. Tears welled up in my eyes. I didn't want Mrs. Winslow to see them. I couldn't tell her that I was afraid Sunny and I might never be friends again. So I changed the subject by telling her that we were all going crazy trying to come up with a name for the baby. Some of Jeff's silly ideas made her laugh. Then she started coughing this awful raspy cough, which made her throw up. After we cleaned up, she lay back on the pillows.

I told her I thought I should go so she could rest.

"Maybe," she murmured. "Sunny's too busy to come today, but Paul will be here after he closes the bookstore."

I told her that I was going to the bookstore to buy some books and magazines for Carol. She said I should ask Mr. Winslow for a copy of a book called _Name Your Baby_. As a gift from her to Carol.

She smiled weakly. "The next time you come you can give me an update on your quest for the perfect baby name," she said. "I'm looking forward to the baby's arrival. If we're lucky the baby will look just like you."

I kissed her good-bye.

I don't think there's much chance that the baby will look like me. But it was sweet of Mrs. Winslow to say that. It's just like her to think of everybody but herself.

It's too bad Sunny can't be more like her mother.

I took a bus into town and went directly to the bookstore. Mr. Winslow is expanding it. It's been really stressful, especially with Mrs. Winslow so sick. Sunny helps her father out occasionally — but she always complains about it. She got Ducky a job at the store too. I think Sunny wants to keep her <u>chauffeur</u> close by.

Mr. Winslow was deep in conference with Ducky about where some books had to be shelved. I asked another clerk where the magazines were.

"By the fiction," she answered.

As I was looking through the latest issue of _Vogue_, I heard Sunny's laugh.

It never occurred to me that she'd be there. Since she'd cut school, I figured she was at Venice Beach for the day. Now here she was. A magazine rack away from me. Hanging over some guy's shoulder as he flipped through a car magazine.

"Cool," she said. "That's the hottest car. Cool and hot. Perfect."

"I'm going to test-drive it later," he told her. "I know the salesman. He'll let me take it out alone. I could come by and give you a turn in it. What do you say?"

"I say okay," Sunny answered. "Just pull into the driveway and honk twice."

The guy closed the magazine and grinned at her.

I thought, _Sunny, if you have time to ride around with some guy you hardly know, you have plenty of time to visit your mother._ Then I remembered my resolution to be like Ducky and hang in there for my friend. I decided that if Sunny made a gesture of friendship to me, even a little smile, I would talk to her. I'd say that I knew this was a hard time for her. Maybe I could tell her that her mother needed her.

The guy left. Sunny smiled to herself. Then I saw the corners of her mouth go down and an incredibly sad look come over her face. She looked sad and very lonely, like when we first found out that her mother had cancer. <u>This is the moment</u>, I thought, <u>this is the moment to make up with her.</u>

I was just about to say her name when she turned and saw me. Her sad expression turned to anger. "What are <u>you</u> doing?" she hissed. "Spying on me? Just mind your own business, okay? And <u>leave me alone</u>."

In a heartbeat I felt my sympathy turn to anger. "I was not . . ." I started to say. But Sunny had already turned her back on me and headed toward the rear exit.

The end.

Thursday night 6/11
I haven't had time to write. Too busy studying for exams and helping take care of

Carol. Endless errands. Carol is bored and restless. I don't blame her. I would be too if I was trapped in bed for three months. I'm bored enough just keeping her company.

These days Carol has two topics of conversation. One: what to name the baby. Two: what she's going to do when she's "back on her feet." I don't think she realizes that Baby No-Name is going to take up most of her time when she's back on her feet. Yesterday she made me pick up the summer class schedule at her gym and the new issue of <u>Rollerblade</u> magazine. Carol can't do the normal things a pregnant woman does, like shop for baby clothes and decorate the baby's room. I'm the one who has to do those things.

Tomorrow I have to go to the mall after school and get the baby's layette — all the things he or she will need for the first six months.

Dad and I are spending the weekend painting, decorating, and putting together the furniture for the baby's room. Carol has a whole file of ideas of how she wants the room to look, which she's cut out of magazines.

Maggie thinks it's cute that I'm doing all this. She and Ducky are going with me to the mall. Amalia might come too. Thank goodness I have some friends left.

WHEN AM I GOING TO STUDY FOR FINALS?

Friday afternoon 6/12

Here I am at the juice bar at the mall. There are three big shopping bags at my feet — pale yellow bags with pink and blue block lettering that says BABY BOUTIQUE. Maggie and Amalia are at the music store, and Ducky went to pick up Sunny at the beach and drop her off at the hospital. He asked me if I wanted to go with him. So I can be verbally abused by Sunny? No thank you.

Shopping for baby clothes was worse than I'd imagined. Not because of the baby and not because of the clothes. Because of guys.

They drive me crazy (not Ducky). They can be so immature.

When we got to the mall we checked out a few of our favorite clothing stores. Finally, I pulled out the list of things for the baby.

Maggie read it over my shoulder. "There's a lot of stuff here," she commented. "Are you sure Carol's not having twins?"

I was laughing, but I said, "That's not funny. I can't imagine our life with even one baby."

"It'll be fun," said Amalia. "I love my sister."

"But your sister is older than you," I pointed out. "When I'm twenty-one, the baby — who is going to be my _half_ sister or brother — will only be eight. We're different generations."

"It'll be like you're her second mother," Ducky said brightly.

"I'm thirteen!" I shrieked. "I don't want to be _anybody's_ mother — first _or_ second."

I turned to Maggie, but she was

looking at herself in the store window. I checked myself out too. I looked like your average kid. Straggly blonde hair, a plain white T-shirt tucked in my jeans, a knapsack slung over one shoulder. Maggie looked like a <u>sophisticated</u> kid in a black linen miniskirt, scoop-neck purple T-shirt, blue suede sandals, and a trendy short haircut. Our eyes met in our reflections.

I was about to tell her how I felt about my dad starting a new family, when she said, "I wish I'd worn my burgundy dress today. It's more flattering."

"You look great!" I told her. (She did.)

"My stomach sticks out. They'll think I'm pregnant in that store." She slapped her stomach like she was angry at it.

"You do <u>not</u> look pregnant," Amalia commented.

"I'm going to lose five pounds," Maggie said.

"Five pounds!" I protested. "You look perfect just the way you are."

"No I don't," Maggie snapped.

"But Maggie . . ." I started to say.

"Thin is in," said Maggie.

"She's right about that," agreed Ducky. "Most of the models look weak and sort of sickly."

"You and I are the same height," I told her. "If you need to lose five pounds, what do you think about me?"

Maggie put her left hand around her right wrist. "Look at this," she said. "Small bones." Her index finger overlapped her thumb. Next, she put her hand around my wrist. There was no overlapping. "You have larger bones," she said. "I should weigh a lot less than you do because my bones are smaller."

I gave up.

"Come on. Let's go to the baby store," I said.

I'm worried about Maggie. And I'm disappointed in her as a friend. Anytime I've tried to talk to her about my problems, she starts talking about her weight, which is definitely not a problem.

We went into Baby Boutique.

"It smells great in here," Amalia said.

"Like baby powder," I added.

"And look at the shopping carts," Ducky said as he rolled one toward Maggie. "They're baby carriages!"

"Cute," Maggie commented. "All _very_ cute." She pushed it toward me. "It's your baby. You can push it."

"It's not going to be _my_ baby," I protested.

I pushed the carriage/shopping cart down the aisle. It was hard to believe that whatever was in Carol's belly would soon be in a baby carriage.

"Look at this," Amalia cooed. "Isn't it adorable?" She held up the tiniest orange T-shirt I'd ever seen. In purple lettering it announced, "I'm here!" Amalia insisted I should get it for the baby. I told her it was cute — but I figured I'd just stick to what was on the list.

We were standing at the front desk waiting to check out. The salesclerk was helping a _very_ pregnant woman with her shopping list.

Amalia was holding up an infant nightie. She laid it against Ducky's chest.

"Imagine, Ducky, you were this tiny once."

Ducky wasn't paying attention. He was looking at the doorway. I saw his expression transform from happy to fearful to annoyed in a split second.

Two Cro Mags — Marco and Mad Moose — took a few steps into the store.

"Isn't that sweet?" said Marco.

"Ducky and his girls," said Mad Moose.

"Just ignore them," Ducky whispered between clenched teeth.

"I wonder which one of them is pregnant," Marco said.

"Ducky couldn't be the father," Mad Moose added.

"Clear out," Ducky called to them.

"Get a life," added Amalia.

Mad Moose shouted, "Maybe _Ducky's_ the one who's pregnant." They roared with laughter and finally left.

Typical Cro Mag humor — not funny and at someone else's expense.

"Jerks," Ducky mumbled. "I can't

believe I used to hang out with some of those guys in sixth grade."

I could tell he was upset. He looked at his watch. "I have to pick up Sunny. I'll be back to get you guys in about an hour."

"Great," said Amalia. She gave him a kiss on the cheek. "Thanks, Ducky."

"I'm sorry I dragged you in here," I told him.

He grinned at me. "I had fun. Don't let those creeps get you down."

Just like Ducky. Worrying about us when he's the one who's most hurt.

Friday night 6/12

I was nervous while we were waiting for Ducky to pick us up in front of the mall. What if Sunny was with him? What if she had decided to go to the hospital later or not at all? Would I be sitting in the backseat next to her? I didn't know what I would do or say. Just imagining the scene made me feel angry at Sunny.

Fortunately, Ducky was alone.

As we rode along, Amalia and Maggie sang one song after another, so I didn't notice how quiet Ducky was until after he had dropped them off at Amalia's house and we were alone in the car.

I told him I was sorry that I had dragged him to the mall. That if I'd known he had to pick up Sunny I would have taken the bus. He said he drove us because he wanted to come with us.

"Well, those guys in the store —" I started to say.

"That's not what's bothering me," he said.

"Is it Alex?" I asked.

He shook his head.

"Then process of elimination tells me it's Sunny. You're upset about something she said or did."

"It's all right. Sunny's upset about her mother."

"You should say something to her, Ducky. Don't let her get away with things."

Ducky shrugged. "I don't want to dump on her."

"I don't want to dump on her either, but I'm not going to be her doormat."

"Is that what you think I am?" he asked. "Sunny's doormat?" I could hear the hurt in his voice, and I felt terrible.

We pulled up in front of my house. "I'm sorry," I said. "I didn't mean it that way, Ducky. I just get so frustrated with her."

"That's all right."

We were both looking at Sunny's house.

"The way Sunny's been acting has to be harder on you than it is on me. You've been friends for so long."

I nodded. "And we used to be so close, Ducky. I really miss that closeness." I put my hand over his arm. "I admire you. You're so loyal to Alex and Sunny. I just can't be like that and it's frustrating."

To my surprise, Ducky replied, "Sometimes I do think I'm like a doormat. That I let everyone walk all over me. I could use a good sweep."

I told him that he was a good friend to a lot of people, but that he should be a good friend to himself too. Then I said I better go in.

Neither of us moved.

"So you're going to be busy all day tomorrow with the baby's room," he said. "It can't be all that much fun for you. Are you and Carol very close?"

I told him how immature Carol seems to me. How sometimes we get on each other's nerves.

Ducky said that's pretty normal. I was glad he understood. His one piece of advice was to not let my feelings for Carol (or lack of them) color how I feel about the baby.

"You must miss talking to Sunny about this stuff," Ducky observed. "I think you're angry at her for not being there for you. Just when you need her."

I told him I hadn't thought about it like that. But that I was mostly angry at her because she wouldn't let me help her. "She's screwing up all over the place, Ducky."

Ducky nodded. "It's rough. But I predict it will all work out in time."

"Ducky," I said with a laugh. "You should be a shrink. You would make a great one."

"You think so? I was sure my true calling was the taxi business."

"You could be Shrink-on-wheels," I suggested.

We laughed.

Ducky helped me carry the packages into the house.

True Ducky chivalry.

Noon on Saturday 6/13

Last night and this morning Dad and I painted the spare bedroom. It is now officially known as The Nursery. The Nursery is across the hall from Dad and Carol's room. Carol supervised us from her bed while we worked. We painted the walls a pale, pale yellow and the trim bright white. The room glows.

This afternoon the baby furniture is being delivered. It's all white. The rocker cushions and curtains are blue-and-white-checkered.

The walls look bare, but Carol said as soon as she's "on her feet" she'll pick out some artwork for them.

We ordered pizza for lunch. I paid the delivery guy, then brought a tray with pizza and sodas to Dad and Carol. They didn't see me come in the room. Dad was lying across the bed with his head on Carol's belly. She was stroking his hair. He was humming a lullaby to Belly Baby. I felt like I was an intruder. I put the tray on the bureau and turned to leave.

My dad saw me and sat up. "Aren't you going to eat with us, Dawn?" he asked.

"I better study for exams," I told him. "I'll eat in my room. Call me when the furniture comes."

So here I am, eating pizza and writing in my journal. I'm studying for my math final next.

I miss studying with Sunny. We used to make snacks, lock ourselves in her room, and not leave until we thought we were ready for the test. We had fun and we got our work done. The new Sunny would never

do anything like that. I miss the old Sunny.
I wish she would come back.

Later 6/13

Fabulous news. Maggie's dad just gave
her three tickets to the Flash concert, and
she invited me and Amalia to go with her.
We're sleeping over at Maggie's house
afterward. Maybe Maggie and I can
become better friends. I love Flash.

I am going to get dressed now, try
to forget about Sunny, Belly Baby, exams,
and Stoneybrook — and have some FUN! At
least for one evening . . .

At Maggie's after the concert 6/13

What a night! The concert was fabulous,
extraordinary, GREAT! I'm so wound up
I can't fall asleep.

Even though there are about a thousand
rooms in this house, Amalia and I are
sleeping in Maggie's room. It's a

sleepover, after all. Besides, Maggie's room
is so big the whole eighth grade could stay
there. At the moment, though, I'm in the
living room (one of them), writing about
what happened tonight.

First of all, we met at Maggie's.

"My dad's still at work and he has the
tickets," Maggie explained. "But Reg drove
over to pick them up. He'll be back for
us." (Reg is the Blumes' new chauffeur.)

"I should say hello to your mother,"
I told Maggie.

"She's by the pool."

Before we went out to the pool, Pilar,
the Blumes' maid, offered us fresh-
squeezed orange juice. Amalia and I both
took a glass.

"Don't you want some?" I asked
Maggie.

"I just ate," she said. "I'm full."

Mrs. Blume was sitting on a lounge
chair next to another woman, who turned out
to be the actor Mel Rand's wife. Famous
people are always hanging out at the
Blumes', so I'm used to it. Amalia, who
hasn't been around the Blumes that long,

was very cool about meeting Mrs. Rand, which shows how cool _she_ is. Mrs. Blume loved my dress (borrowed from Carol's prematernity wardrobe, I must admit) and couldn't stop raving about Amalia's hair. "I know a woman who spends two hundred dollars every four weeks to _try_ to have color like that," she told us.

Maggie had this frozen smile on her face. She always seems uncomfortable around her mom. And in her fancy house. It's like she's embarrassed by everything. Some kids at school think having a lot of money is a big deal. Maggie does not like this. Which I can understand.

"It's seven-thirty," Maggie told us. "We better go."

"You girls have some of the best seats in the house," Maggie's mother gushed. "Just show your tickets and mention your father's name, and you won't have to deal with the crowds."

I wonder if Mrs. Blume is one of those people who judge other people by how much money they have.

"Thanks, Mrs. Blume," Amalia said.

"See you later," I added.

We headed back to the house. "Have a ball, girls," Mrs. Blume called after us. "And Maggie, ask Pilar to bring us out another pitcher of gin and tonics."

I saw Maggie flinch when her mother said that. I've noticed that Mrs. Blume drinks a lot, even during the day. I wonder how much it bothers Maggie.

Maggie hates being driven around in her dad's limousine. But I love it. Amalia seemed to be enjoying it too, but she didn't make a big deal about it. I think she knows how Maggie feels about things.

Maggie hasn't actually <u>talked</u> to me about how she feels. That isn't Maggie's way. But it's pretty easy to figure out how she feels about the limo. For example, she asked Reg to drop us off two blocks from the stadium. Which, of course, was because she didn't want anyone to see her get out of the limo.

We didn't try to go in ahead of everybody else. I was glad. Half the fun of a concert is being part of the crowd going in. But I must admit it was great to have seats close to the stage. For two and a half hours I forgot about everything except the music.

Reg met us where he'd dropped us off. The crowd from the concert had spilled out into the surrounding blocks, so we couldn't exactly hide the fact that we were getting into a limo. A pack of guys was staring at us.

One of them shouted, "Take me with you — aw, come on."

"Please, pretty please," added another. "We'll be good."

"Right!" shouted a third. "_Real_ good."

We ignored them.

As Reg pulled the car away from the curb, Maggie mumbled, "I hate that my dad makes me use his car."

"It must be hard," I said, glancing at Maggie. But she dropped the subject.

Mrs. Blume was waiting up for us, or maybe she was waiting for Mr. Blume, who still wasn't home from work.

"My father is on a new movie project," Maggie explained.

"He's _always_ on a new movie project," Mrs. Blume commented.

She wanted to know all about the concert. But she didn't seem to listen to what we were saying. I think she had been drinking quite a bit. I kept the conversation rolling until Maggie suggested we get ready for bed.

"I might as well turn in too," Mrs. Blume muttered. "There's food for you girls in the kitchen. Pilar made a late supper for you."

Amalia and I ate big helpings of Pilar's sesame noodles, tofu salad, and blueberry pie. Pilar is a fabulous cook. But all Maggie had was a glass of water, about four strands of sesame noodles, and a few blueberries that she picked out of the pie. "I ate before the concert," she said.

"Me too," I told her. "But that was hours ago."

"I don't like to eat late," she said. End of subject.

Maggie's father came home while we were eating. He wanted to know all about the concert and really paid attention to what we said. Amalia and I thanked him for the tickets.

He turned to Maggie. "When you're working in my office this summer, Rod Flash will be coming in. He's doing a number for the sound track for the new film. You'll meet him. I've already told him you're a musician."

"_Dad_ —" Maggie protested.

He ignored her and kept talking. "I'll ask him to tell you how he got started in the business and give you a couple of singing lessons."

"But Dad," said Maggie, "I don't want lessons from him. I like Mrs. Knudsen."

Mr. Blume acted like he hadn't even heard what Maggie said. "By the way," he went on, "have your mother help you pick out some clothes to wear to the office. She knows what to do in that regard." He laughed. "She should, with the credit card charges she makes."

"Dad, I have —" Maggie started to say, but Mr. Blume interrupted her again.

"I know, I know. You can figure out

what to wear all on your own. You're right. I trust your judgment. But don't hold back. Get whatever you want. You should look perfect for your first real job." He stood up and kissed her on the head. "I'm looking forward to showing you the ropes. My chip off the old block."

Maggie looked incredibly sad after he left.

Amalia and I put our dishes in the sink and we all went to Maggie's room. We didn't stay up talking. Amalia fell asleep right away. Maggie stayed in the bathroom for a really long time. I noticed she took her journal in with her and I heard her humming quietly to herself. Some soulful tune. I figured she was writing a song.

When she came out I whispered, "Did you write a new song?"

She nodded.

"Sing it for me. I'd love to hear it."

"It needs some more work."

"Do you want to talk about what happened tonight?" I asked. "In the kitchen."

"What about it?"

"You didn't seem very excited about working in your father's office."

"Oh, that," Maggie said. "I'm not really interested in the film business."

"Maybe you could tell him that," I said.

"It's no big deal. I'd rather not talk about it." She got into bed. "Sweet dreams."

"'Night, Maggie," I whispered.

I'm hurt that Maggie won't open up to me. Not surprised, really — but still hurt. Sure, I was closer to Sunny than I was to Maggie. But with Sunny out of the picture, I thought Maggie and I would become closer friends. Now that I think about it, Sunny and I were always much closer to each other than to Maggie. I can't remember that Maggie ever opened up to any of us.

I'm beginning to think that Maggie isn't very close to anyone, even Amalia.

Now I can't sleep. All the things that were bothering me before the concert have come back one by one. I am going to have to study for exams all day tomorrow. Finals start on Monday. I wish I could talk to Sunny about Maggie. I wish I could talk to Sunny about _anything._

Wednesday 6/17

What is wrong with me? Why am I so angry at Sunny?

Here's what happened.

I studied like crazy for my math final. I felt that I was ready.

"Well, _I'm_ not ready," Maggie said as we walked into our math classroom. "My mother made me go shopping yesterday afternoon. I only studied for four hours."

I didn't study for four hours and I thought I'd studied a lot. I knew that Maggie would ace the math final and I told her so. She still looked worried but changed the subject by asking if I thought Sunny would show up for the exam. I told her I didn't know, but that even if Sunny did take the final I didn't see how she could pass math. Not with all the classes she's cut.

We took our seats. I put out two sharp pencils, folded my hands, and waited for the exam to begin. If Sunny didn't take any of her finals she'd fail the year. She'd have to repeat eighth grade. We wouldn't graduate from Vista together.

I thought about the plans we'd made for after high school graduation. We had been talking about them for years. First we wanted to spend the summer in Europe. Then we'd go to the same college, hopefully as roommates. I really believed we would do those things. They were our shared dreams. Well, they used to be.

I turned my attention to Ms. Whalen, who was giving her final instructions before passing out the exam.

That's the moment Sunny walked in the room. As she passed me to go to her seat, we made eye contact. She smiled. It was a sarcastic smile, more like a smirk, that said, "You didn't think I'd show up, and here I am."

I didn't know how to respond, so I looked down at my desk.

Then I thought, <u>Did I read the wrong</u>

thing into Sunny's look? Maybe the smile wasn't _meant_ to be sarcastic. Maybe she was reaching out to me. I decided the next time we passed each other I'd be the first to smile — a real smile. I'd see how she responded.

Sunny finished the exam early and left the room before I did.

I thought about Sunny as I fiddled with my locker.

Then I felt a tap on my shoulder.

I turned around with a big smile on my face.

There stood Jill.

"Uh, hi," I said.

"Hi," said Jill. She was wearing a pink sweatshirt with a big picture of the head of a boxer dog on it. It read, "I ♡ my boxer." Inwardly I groaned. Sunny and I had given it to Jill for her eleventh birthday.

I sighed. Maybe I was acting childish by being so critical about how someone dresses.

"How are you doing?" Jill asked.

"Okay," I said.

I couldn't believe Jill was talking to me. We'd barely spoken to each other in months.

"The math exam was hard," Jill commented.

"Yeah," I agreed.

"How's Carol? I mean with the baby and everything. Isn't it time for it to be born?"

Maybe that was it. Jill wanted to know about Carol's pregnancy. Jill loves babies. I told her that Carol was due any day.

"That is so great," she gushed. "You must be so excited."

"It is pretty exciting."

There is no way Jill would understand that I was _not_ thrilled about the baby. Still, I found that I didn't feel angry at Jill anymore. I actually felt a little sorry for her. She thinks I don't hang out with her anymore because of the Carol-is-pregnant incident, when it is about so much more than that. I felt a little guilty about how I'd been treating her lately. I guess that's why I found myself inviting her out for a soda.

"Sure," said Jill with a giggle.

We walked out of school together.

"So . . . how's Carol feeling and everything? She must be big," said Jill.

I told her that Carol was bedridden. Next, Jill said she'd heard about the fire. "No wonder you're angry at Sunny," she continued. "I wouldn't talk to her either."

I told her it was more complicated than that but didn't try to explain.

Jill said, "I know what you mean. Sunny's acting so wild and hangs out with all these older guys. Do those guys go to her house?" Jill's eyes were sparkling.

I told her I didn't spy on Sunny and changed the subject by asking about Jill's dogs — Spike, Shakespeare, and Smee. Unfortunately, none of them are as cute as the boxer on Jill's shirt. But she loves them and can talk about them endlessly. Which she did.

While we had sodas I told Jill some of the names Carol and my dad were considering for the baby. I also told her they didn't want to find out the sex.

"I think that's cute," Jill gushed. "I

wouldn't want to know either." So like Jill. But I didn't mind that much. I guess that shows how desperate I am for a friend.

I wonder if I'll ever have a best friend again.

I can't believe how fast the time flies. I've been sitting on this park bench for an hour writing in my journal. I better go home and help entertain Carol.

What a day.

When I got home I had an eerie feeling something was wrong. It was too quiet. No music or television sounds coming from Carol's room. No video game sounds from the living room. No Mrs. Bruen calling from the kitchen, "Is that you, Dawn?"

I ran to Carol's room. Her bed was empty and unmade. I knew that Mrs. Bruen wouldn't leave a room looking like that unless it was an emergency.

I thought, <u>Carol must be at the hospital.</u> <u>I should look for a note.</u>

I flew down the stairs and into the kitchen.

There was a note all right:

"Baby on the way. We've called the ambulance. We're going to the hospital. Your father will meet us there. Mrs. B."

I was excited and nervous. The baby was being born. Maybe right that minute! But Carol was going to the hospital in an ambulance. What was wrong? I wanted to be at the hospital with everyone else. I had to know what was happening. I would go crazy if I waited at home alone.

I looked out the window toward Sunny's house. Mr. Winslow's car wasn't there. I thought, Ducky. I'll call him.

But Ducky wasn't home.

I had to get to the hospital. Fast. The only person I could think to call was Maggie. Luckily, she was home.

"This is so exciting!" she yelled. "You have to go to the hospital. Reg and I will pick you up in fifteen minutes."

Twenty-five minutes later we pulled up in front of the hospital. Reg told Maggie that her father didn't need him until ten o'clock, that he would wait for us in the parking lot.

I knew my way around the hospital from all my visits to Mrs. Winslow, so I led the way to the maternity wing on the third floor. As we passed the nursery window, I looked in. The newborns were lined up in rows of little cribs. Two were in incubators. Was one of them my half brother or half sister?

"We're looking for Carol Olson," I told an attendant standing at the nursing station.

"Her family is in the waiting room at the end of the hall," she said.

My heart was pounding. It was hard not to run down the hall.

Mrs. Bruen and Jeff were the only ones in the waiting room. Mrs. Bruen was pacing back and forth. Jeff was looking out the window.

"What happened?" I asked. "Are they okay?"

"Everything seems to be going according to schedule," said Mrs. Bruen. "Poor thing. All she must be going through."

I hadn't thought much about the actual <u>birth</u> of the baby, that it was going to be difficult for Carol.

Mrs. Bruen put her hand on my shoulder. "But don't worry, Dawn. Carol will be fine. And so will the baby."

"You came in Maggie's limo, didn't you?" Jeff asked. He pointed to the parking lot. "That's it down there. Can I go for a ride?" he begged. "Can I, Maggie?"

"Not now, Jeff," Maggie told him.

"Where's Dad?" I asked.

"With Carol, of course," Mrs. Bruen said.

Of course.

We hung out in the waiting room for two hours. Mrs. Bruen and Jeff worked on a jigsaw puzzle of a sailboat that some other nervous family had started. Maggie and I reviewed biology. Maggie had been smart enough to bring her book along. But it was hard to study and worry about Carol and the baby at the same time. I did my share of pacing.

Finally, my father came bursting into the waiting room. He was beaming. "It's — a — girl!" he said in a choked voice. His eyes gleamed. I've never seen him look so happy. "She's beautiful. She's fine. Carol too. They came through with flying colors." Tears spilled down his cheeks. I have never seen my father so happy that he cried. Never. Not even the day he and Carol were married.

"A girl?!" Jeff exclaimed. "I thought it was going to be a boy. I didn't think of any girl names!"

Dad tousled Jeff's hair and wrapped us both in a big hug. I cried too.

But my tears of happiness were for Dad, not for myself.

Dad suggested that the rest of us go home and have some dinner while Carol and the baby rested. Then we should come back to the hospital in a couple of hours. "I want you to meet your sister," he said.

Half sister, I thought.

"Can I go with Maggie in the limo?" Jeff asked anyone who would listen. "Can I?"

Mrs. Bruen said Jeff and I could

both go with Maggie and that she would meet us at home. For the moment, Jeff was more excited about the limo than he was about our baby half sister, No Name.

After Maggie dropped us off, I came up here to my room to write. I can see Sunny's bedroom window from my desk. It is so weird not to call her with the news. I guess Dad will tell Mr. Winslow and he'll tell Sunny. Weird and sad.

11 p.m. 6/17

We rushed through dinner so we could go right back to the hospital. I brought Carol her Discman and some of her favorite CDs. Mrs. Bruen picked flowers from the garden for her. And Jeff remembered to bring the baby name book. So we could pick out a girl's name.

As we walked through the maternity floor we stopped to look in at the newborns. Now one of them would be Baby Schafer-Olson. We read all of the names, even the ones on the incubators. None said "Schafer-Olson."

Mrs. Bruen and I exchanged a worried glance. Had something happened to Baby Schafer-Olson? We rushed to Room 307.

There, lying in Carol's arms, was the baby we were looking for.

"Hi," I whispered to Carol and Dad.

"You don't have to whisper," Dad said in a loud, happy voice. "We want her to get used to noise."

"Come on over and see her," Carol said. Carol looked tired but so very happy.

I looked down at the sweetest infant I'd ever seen. Dad put his arm around me. "You know what, Sunshine?" he asked. Dad hadn't called me that in so long. The tone of his voice was warm and familiar. It was the voice he used to tell me bedtime stories when I was little and that he used to comfort me when I was sad. I suppose he'll use that voice with his new daughter. It's her turn to have bedtime stories and a dad who makes up a terrific nickname for her.

Hearing Dad call me Sunshine reminded me of Sunny too. The fact that my nickname was Sunny's real name was the great coincidence of our friendship. Not many people are named Sunshine. We decided this was a sign that we were supposed to be best friends forever.

I missed being Dad's Sunshine and I missed Sunny. I felt a knot rise up in my throat, as if I was going to cry.

I swallowed and said, "What, Dad?"

"Your sister looks just like you did."

"But . . ." I looked at Carol. It was Carol's baby. Shouldn't she look like Carol?

"She does look like you," said Carol. "I've seen your baby pictures, Dawn. Isn't it wonderful?"

I am amazed that Carol doesn't mind that her baby looks like me. She lifted the baby and held her out to me. "Here."

I took my half sister and cradled her carefully in the crook of my left arm. Other newborns I've seen looked scrunched up, like old men. But not this baby. She has smooth, soft, pink skin. And her lips are a perfect tulip shape.

"She's so little!" Jeff exclaimed. "I thought she'd be bigger. Are boys bigger?"

My father laughed. "No," he said. "And Elizabeth Grace is eight pounds, two ounces, which is a very respectable weight for a girl or a boy."

"Elizabeth Grace!" Jeff cried. He threw the "name your baby" book down on Carol's bed and pouted. "You went ahead and named her without me."

"I'm sorry, Jeff," Dad said. "But it just came to us. We were looking at her and I said, 'Let's call her Elizabeth.'"

"And I was thinking what a grace it was that she is finally here," Carol said. "That she is my special Grace. We put them together and came up with Elizabeth Grace."

"You can give her a nickname," Dad told Jeff.

"Like Liz, maybe," Carol suggested. "Or Lizzy."

Jeff thought for a few seconds. "I'm going to call her Gracie," he announced. "That's my name for her."

"Gracie," Carol and Dad said in unison.

My dad looked at me and I nodded. I

thought Gracie was a perfect nickname for
Elizabeth Grace.

"I like it," said Dad.

"Me too," Carol added.

"She is so lovely, Carol," Mrs. Bruen
said. "Now, wasn't it worth all those months
in bed?"

"Yes, it was," Carol said. "You were
right."

I felt as if I were dreaming. I
couldn't take my eyes off the peaceful infant
in my arms. "Elizabeth Grace," I
whispered. "Happy birthday."

Then we all sang "Happy Birthday" to
the newest member of our family.

I'm too tired to study for my finals. I
have all day tomorrow to study. I'll go to
the hospital too. I want to visit Mrs.
Winslow when I'm there. I promised to
tell her all about the baby after she was
born.

There's also something else I want to do
with Mrs. Winslow. I hope it works.

It was hard to study this morning. Dad was calling all our friends and relatives to tell them about Elizabeth Grace. A lot of them wanted to talk to me. I guess they were worried that I'd be jealous, which is pretty weird since I'm thirteen years old. When Dad wasn't on the phone, it was ringing with congratulations from people who had heard about the baby from the people he had called.

Around noon, Dad and I drove to the hospital together. "After I see Carol and Gracie," he said, "I have to drop in at the office for a couple of hours. Mrs. Bruen is coming over this afternoon. She can give you a ride home."

"Perfect," I said. "I want to have time to visit Mrs. Winslow too."

Dad was going straight to maternity on the third floor, but I got off the elevator at the cancer care unit on the second floor. There were no excited fathers on the second floor. No glowing mothers. No newborns. I walked down the hall past rooms of very sick and dying people. A shiver went down my spine and I felt overwhelmingly sad.

On this floor people were fighting for their lives. Some of them would die. Their loved ones were helping them leave the world. On the third floor infants were being helped into the world.

I took a deep breath, put a smile on my face, and walked into Mrs. Winslow's room.

She was sitting up in a chair looking out the window. "Hi," I said softly. She turned to me. Two little tubes came out of her nostrils and were connected to an oxygen tank. "Sun - Dawn," she said. "Hi. At first I thought you were Sunny."

"I have good news," I told her.

"The baby?"

I nodded. Then I sat on the edge of the bed and told her everything. I realized that Mr. Winslow had told her Gracie had been born but still she wanted to know every one of _my_ details.

"I love newborns," she told me. "I always wanted more children. There was one miscarriage after Sunny. Then no more pregnancies." She smiled. "I was very blessed to have Sunny."

I thought angrily that Sunny wasn't much of a blessing to anyone these days. But I pushed the thought away. I didn't want <u>any</u> negative energy in Mrs. Winslow's room.

Mrs. Winslow reached over and patted my hand. "Tell me again what the baby looks like."

The skin on Mrs. Winslow's hand and arm was transparent and wrinkled. She was very thin. I thought of the expression "skin and bones."

"Okay," I said. "But I think I can do better than that. I want to take you to see her."

For an instant Mrs. Winslow looked excited by the idea. Then a cloud passed over her face. "Oh, I can't go," she said.

"I bet the nurses would let you."

"It'll be so depressing for Carol and everyone. I mean, it's such a <u>happy</u> time for them. They don't want to see me."

My heart ached for Mrs. Winslow. She was worried about everyone but herself.

"Don't say that," I said. "Don't even

think it. I _want_ you to see Gracie. And you said yourself that you love newborns." I stood up. "Let me at least ask the nurses, okay?"

A big smile erupted on Mrs. Winslow's face. A familiar twinkle came into her eyes. "Dawn, I can't think of anything I'd rather do today than meet Elizabeth Grace Schafer-Olson," she said.

Her face was beautiful. She was beautiful. I thought, A person's beauty is deep inside. It is even deeper than good health.

We got permission right away from a nurse, who hurried off to find a wheelchair. I helped Mrs. Winslow get ready for our visit. She put on the bright blue silk robe Mr. Winslow and Sunny had given her for her birthday in April. She ran her hand over the shiny fabric. "Isn't it beautiful?" she asked. "I love wonderful fabrics."

She was practically bald from the chemotherapy, so she decided to cover her head with a scarf. She picked out a pink-and-yellow-striped one from the stack of scarves she'd brought with her to the hospital. She wrapped it around her head and I tied it in a fancy knot at the nape of her neck.

Next, she dabbed some powder on her cheeks. I held up her air tubes while she applied some pink lipstick. Finally, I helped her into the wheelchair.

"Ready?" I said.

"Ready!" she answered. She smiled up at me. "Thank you, Dawn."

I wheeled Mrs. Winslow onto the elevator and we took the short ride to the third floor.

We stopped at the nursery window. Baby Schafer—Olson was in the first row, asleep with her fists on her chest.

I pointed. "There she is."

After a few seconds Mrs. Winslow whispered, "She's perfect. Just perfect."

"Isn't she?" said a male voice. I looked up. It was my dad. He leaned over and kissed Mrs. Winslow on the cheek. "Isn't this something, Betsy?" he asked.

Mrs. Winslow had tears in her eyes. Happy tears. "Yes it is," she said.

"Something very wonderful. Congratulations."

"Carol's sleeping," he said. "That's why they put the baby back here."

While Dad and Mrs. Winslow talked, I signaled to the maternity nurse. I explained to her that Mrs. Winslow was a patient on the second floor and a close friend of our family. "Could she hold my sister?" I asked.

"I don't see why not," said the nurse. "Wheel your friend over here to the door and I'll get the baby."

After Dad left I told Mrs. Winslow, "You can hold her."

"Really?"

I nodded.

"I'd love that," she said.

I wheeled Mrs. Winslow to the doorway and the nurse handed me Elizabeth Grace. I put her in Mrs. Winslow's arms. "Oh, look at her," she said softly. "How precious." She took Elizabeth Grace's fist, gently opened it, and put her thin finger in the tiny palm of the baby's hand. That one-day-old hand closed around Mrs. Winslow's finger.

"Hello, my little namesake," Mrs. Winslow said.

That's when I realized it. Mrs. Winslow's name — Betsy — was a nickname for Elizabeth. I don't think my dad had named Elizabeth after Mrs. Winslow, not consciously anyway. But I was so glad that was the baby's name. I felt incredibly happy and sad at the same time. Happy that my sister would go through her life with Elizabeth Winslow's name. And sad that Elizabeth Winslow wouldn't see her namesake and newest neighbor grow up. I squatted beside the wheelchair and whispered to Mrs. Winslow, "I love you."

She smiled at me. "I love you, Dawn. You're like a second daughter to me. Thank you so much for bringing me up here."

"Thank _you_," I said.

"I should go back to my room. I need to lie down."

I took Elizabeth Grace from Elizabeth Winslow and gave the baby back to the nurse. Then I wheeled Mrs. Winslow to the elevator and to her room on the second floor.

Friday morning 6/19

I'm waiting for the biology exam to begin. English final this afternoon. I hope I can concentrate enough to finish.

I couldn't believe what my friends did for me today.

It started when Jill met me outside school. She'd been waiting for me. "I heard about the baby!" she said excitedly. She said how glad she was that it was a girl and handed me a box wrapped in pink foil with a huge silver ribbon. "Open it," she said. I did. Gracie's present was a stuffed dog — a boxer. I thought it was sweet that Jill had gone to all this trouble when we barely saw each other anymore. I told her about Elizabeth Grace as we walked into school. Our lockers are in different halls, so we separated in the main lobby. But first Jill gave me a hug and congratulated me again.

When I reached my locker I had an even bigger surprise. My friends had posted a sign on the door that said, IT'S A LITTLE SISTER! A dozen pink helium balloons were tied to my locker handle with curly purple and silver ribbons.

Loads of people gathered around my locker and asked questions. I didn't even care that the Cro Mags who walked by yelled out dumb things like, "She didn't look pregnant to me."

Ducky, Maggie, and Amalia had presents for Elizabeth Grace too. Ducky gave her the T-shirt we'd seen at Baby Boutique — the orange one that said "I'm here!" Maggie gave her a beautiful mobile of brightly colored fish. "I know she'll be a water baby like you," she explained.

I had just opened Maggie's present when Sunny sauntered by, arm in arm with some hunk from the senior class. When they passed my locker she didn't even look at me. I tried to forget about Sunny and concentrate on the gift Amalia handed me. But I couldn't. Sunny had just passed up the perfect opportunity to mend our friendship. All she had to do was give me a friendly look. I wasn't expecting presents, just a smile. I would have smiled back.

It could have been the beginning of the end of our fight.

Maggie tugged on my sleeve. "Open it," she said. I pulled off the rest of the wrapping paper and saw Amalia's gift — a cartoon she had drawn of me and a baby on surfboards. The baby is on a little surfboard and wearing nothing but a diaper. And the drawing of me actually looks like me. Amalia is so talented.

I wonder if I will surf with Elizabeth some day. When she's fifteen, I'll be twenty-eight. Will Elizabeth baby-sit for my children? Wow! That is a weird thought. No wonder I can't concentrate on finals.

But I have two more to take, starting right now. Mrs. Barkley just came in the room.

Friday evening 6/19

Finals are _finally_ over! I'm sure I passed everything, but I don't think my marks will be as high as first semester. I can't worry about it. I'm just glad tests are over and I can focus completely on all the other things that are on my mind — like getting organized to go to Stoneybrook. I can't believe I'm leaving for the summer two days after Carol and Elizabeth come home.

Then there's Maggie. I'm really worried about her — more than ever. Here's what happened today.

After finals Amalia and Maggie met me at my highly decorated locker. Amalia suggested we go for pizza to celebrate the end of finals and the arrival of Gracie.

We practically ran to the pizza parlor. It was mobbed. We found a small table in the back that was meant for two and fit in an extra chair.

"I'm starving," I announced. "I was too worried about the English final to eat much lunch."

"Me too," said Amalia.

Maggie didn't say anything, but I knew she had to be hungry too. All she ate at lunch was a small pile of lettuce and cucumbers from the salad bar with no dressing and one slice of avocado.

When the waitress finally reached us, we ordered a big pie. Half olives — Amalia's choice. And half artichoke hearts — which I know is a favorite of Maggie's. Amalia and I ordered regular colas. Maggie ordered a diet cola. Of course.

"Could you make one of the artichoke slices without cheese, please?" Maggie asked the waitress.

The waitress made a notation on her pad and left.

Amalia and I exchanged a glance. Amalia's expression showed me that she thought Maggie was being very weird about food too. "Maggie," I said. "Pizza without cheese? You've never eaten it that way."

"Cheese is very fattening," Maggie said.

"And delicious," added Amalia. "Plus, it belongs on pizza."

"Is it a crime to want to lose a pound or two?" Maggie asked. She pointed across the room. "Hey, look, there's Ducky and Alex."

Ducky and Alex had just walked through the door. Alex was hanging behind Ducky. Ducky turned to him and said something. Alex shook his head no. Then he turned and walked out. Ducky followed him. Poor Ducky. The end of the school year is supposed to be fun.

Our pizza arrived. It was perfection. Amalia and I were on our second slices when I noticed that Maggie was only halfway through her cheeseless slice.

I had a flashback of four little girls sitting in this same pizza parlor. Sunny and I sat on one side of the booth. Maggie and Jill on the other. We thought we were so grown-up because we were there without any adults. We ordered an extra-large pizza, double cheese. We were carefree and happy and sure that we would be friends forever.

"Maggie, remember the first time you, Jill, Sunny, and I were allowed to go for pizza alone?" I said. "We thought we were so grown-up."

Maggie smiled faintly and nodded. But she was too busy taking a piece of cheese off the edge of her pizza slice to answer.

Amalia and I finished our slices and

Maggie took two more small bites of hers. She stood up. "I'll be right back."

Amalia and I watched her head for the bathroom.

We didn't say anything at first. But after a few seconds we broke the silence by both talking at once.

"You first," I said.

"I was just going to say that Maggie looks thin. I mean, I don't think she needs to lose any more weight."

"I was going to say the same thing."

"Maybe she has a favorite dress or something that she wants to fit into," suggested Amalia.

"Yeah," I said. "Maybe."

I was thinking of Maggie always checking out her reflection in windows and mirrors. And how she used to love food and not worry about every little thing she put in her mouth. But all I said was, "I'm glad Maggie is hanging out with you and the guys in the band."

"Me too. I really like her." Amalia lowered her voice. "Here she comes." We watched Maggie head toward our table.

I wonder if I should say something to Maggie about her weird eating habits. I'm realizing that Maggie is an intense person, always wanting everything to be perfect — perfect grades, perfect music, perfect looks. Now she has this idea that to look perfect she should be thinner, which is totally crazy. Poor Maggie. Why can't she just enjoy life? She has so much going for her. Maybe I should try to talk to her about all this sometime when we're alone. But how can I do that and then disappear on her for the summer?

I just remembered, Maggie never finished that slice of cheeseless pizza.

I'm leaving for Stoneybrook in <u>three</u> days. What am I going to pack? It would be so much easier if I could just bring my whole room with me!

I'll make a list:

* Rollerblades
* ~~Paper-making kit~~
* Book to read on plane
* Three pairs of jeans (blue, black, white)

* Jean shorts
* A zillion T-shirts — long-sleeved
  and short-sleeved. No, that's silly.
  I have clothes in Stoneybrook,
  after all.

I can't do this anymore. I keep
thinking about what I _can't_ take to
Stoneybrook. Mainly people. Here's who I'll
miss most this summer.

* Maggie
* Sunny
* Elizabeth Grace

The strange thing is that none of them
will miss me.

* Maggie won't talk to me about what's
  really important.
* Sunny doesn't talk to me at all.
* Gracie can't talk and is too young to
  know who I am anyway.

I'm going to miss watching Gracie's
first two months on this planet. I already
like her a lot better than I thought I
would. And how can I make up with Sunny
when she's three thousand miles away? This
is so unfair.

Doorbell ringing — gotta go.

Later Friday 6/19

What just happened is so weird I have
to write about it immediately.

I didn't have any idea who could be
ringing the bell. Since I was alone in the
house I said, "Who is it?" before opening
the door.

"Me," a familiar voice answered.
"Sunny."

Sunny ringing our front doorbell? The
same Sunny who always came around to the
kitchen ⬤r and walked right in?

I opened the door. Sunny was standing
there holding a bouquet of flowers.

"I — uh — brought these for Carol,"
she stammered. "From my mother and me.
From Mom's garden."

I looked down at the bouquet. White
daisies, pink and purple cosmos, and yellow
lilies. I remembered when Sunny and I
had helped Mrs. Winslow plant those flowers
after she was diagnosed with lung cancer.

"Come in," I said.

I backed up and Sunny took a few
steps into the house.

My heart was pounding and my mouth

felt dry. Just being near Sunny was making me nervous. I didn't know what to say. I didn't know how to act. Sunny seemed like a stranger to me. The expression on her face, her posture, the way she was dressed . . . even the tone of her voice was unfamiliar.

"So . . . like . . . is Carol here? And the baby?" she asked.

"No," I said. "They have to stay in the hospital an extra day. Because of Carol."

"What's wrong with her?" Sunny asked with alarm.

I told her it was nothing serious, that Carol would be okay and that she and the baby would be coming home the next day. What I wanted to ask Sunny was what had gone wrong with _us_? How had best friends become strangers?

"Hey, well . . . great," said Sunny. "Tell her I said hi. And congratulations."

I thought, _What do you have to say to me, Sunny?_

Sunny pulled on her ear the way she does when she's nervous. She looked around. She hadn't looked at me, really looked me in the eye. But I was avoiding eye contact too.

"You could come back tomorrow," I said. "With the flowers. Or you could bring them to the hospital. Carol would love to see you."

"Okay, I'll do that," said Sunny.

She turned and left. I wanted to say, _Wait. Don't go. We have to talk._ But I didn't have the courage. I stood in the doorway and watched her walk across the lawn. I thought, _If she turns around and looks at me I'll say something._ But what?

I forgive you. I want to be your friend.

No!

How about, _Sunny, do you want to come in for a soda or something?_ Or _How did exams go?_ Or _Do you like working at your father's store?_

All lame.

But it didn't matter.

Sunny didn't turn around.

Now, as I'm writing this, I think I should have said, _Did you hear what they named the baby?_ Or _Guess what? They named the baby Elizabeth Grace. She has the same first name as your mother._

But maybe that wouldn't have been the right thing to say either.

Maybe Sunny and I aren't speaking because we don't know what to say to each other anymore. Or maybe we just don't _have_ anything to say to each other anymore.

I can't believe I've lost my best friend. I feel like _I'm_ lost.

Saturday evening 6/20

Elizabeth Grace is home. We've had loads of visitors and presents today. Carol is so thrilled not to be bedridden that Dad and Mrs. Bruen are afraid she's overdoing it. All her friends squeal when they see the baby. It's a good thing Gracie is already used to a noisy household!

I'm pretty used to babies from baby-sitting so much. I know more about taking care of an infant than Carol does, so I've been helping out. I don't mind, especially now that school is over.

Lots of people besides Dad and Carol say Gracie looks like I did when I was a baby, which means she must look more like Dad's side of the family than Carol's. Whatever. She's here. And she's part of my life. But the fact is, I'm not going to be here for more than two months.

Jeff and I fly to the East Coast Monday at ten in the morning. I better do my laundry and start packing.

Nine weeks is a long time to be gone. I told Dad I was going to miss the baby. He said, "And we'll miss you. But Gracie will be here when you come home. She's not going anywhere." I wonder if he will miss me now that he has _two_ daughters. I think babies take up a lot more love than grown-up daughters. The fact is, babies _need_ their fathers more than grown-up daughters do.

I was thinking about this when Carol came into the kitchen with Gracie on her shoulder.

Carol looked at Dad and me, burst out laughing, and whispered, "You have to go to the baby's room. Jeff just hung a present on her wall."

Jeff yelled from down the hall, "I

hear you laughing, Carol. It's _not_ funny!
It's not a _funny_ present."

Dad and I ran to the baby's room
and Carol followed at a slower pace with
Gracie. On the pale yellow wall was a
brightly colored NBA poster of Michael
Jordan making a slam dunk.

Dad and I exchanged a glance. I
covered my mouth so I wouldn't laugh. Dad
turned a hoot into a cough.

Even so, Jeff could tell that we were
all amused by his gift.

"It's an excellent poster," Jeff wailed.
"I saved my money for it. I sent away for
it and I didn't tell anybody because I
wanted it to be a surprise _for my baby
brother_." He gave my father an angry look.
"Dad, you said I could treat a sister just
the way I'd treat a brother. That she'd
play ball with me and everything. So I'm
giving _her_ the poster even though she's not
a brother." He finished his speech by
mumbling, "But I don't think she's
ever going to be big enough to do
anything."

I love my brother. He's an original.

"Jeff," I said. "You did the best thing. It's a great present."

"And it looks terrific in Gracie's room," said Carol. She looked from Dad to me. "It really does. I love all the colors. And Gracie will too."

"This room <u>was</u> looking a little wimpy," Dad said.

Carol held Gracie out to Jeff. He took her very carefully, held her in the crook of his arm, and faced her toward the poster. "Gracie, that's Michael Jordan," he said. "He's our hero."

Gracie raised her little fist and punched the air as if to say, "<u>All right</u>!"

I better pack.

Sunday / Monday (midnight)

I'm all packed and ready for my summer in Stoneybrook.

I was putting the last things in my suitcase when I heard a soft cry from Gracie's room. I ran down the hall to check on her. Carol and my dad were trying to sleep between feedings. I wanted to quiet Gracie before she woke them up. I lifted her out of her crib and sat in the rocker with her cradled in my arms.

"Did you have a bad dream, little sister?" I whispered. "It happens. But I'm here. I'll make it better." She stopped crying. "I have to go away. But you have a mother and father who adore you." I gently stroked her wisps of soft blonde hair. "I'll be back. We're going to have a wonderful time being sisters. I promise you."

I felt a hand on my shoulder. It startled me, but I realized it was my father before I screamed. I know he overheard me talking to Gracie, but I don't care.

"She's so tiny, Dad," I said.

He sighed. "She's a big responsibility. I can't sleep. I keep waking up to check on her." He reached into his bathrobe pocket and took out a framed picture. "I had this made up for you," he said. "So you'd have it for Stoneybrook."

He held the picture near the night-light

so I could see it better. It was a photo
Dad had taken of me holding Gracie
the day she came home from the hospital.
In it Gracie has on the "I'm here!"
T-shirt.

I smiled up at my father. "Thanks,
Dad."

"I love that photo," he said. "My two
girls. I framed a copy of it for my office
desk too. And I framed a picture for Jeff,
one of him standing with Gracie in front of
the Michael Jordan poster." He handed me
an envelope. "Here are copies of the rest of
the pictures from the roll. I figured you
would want to show them to your mother
and the rest of your Stoneybrook family and
friends."

"That's perfect, Dad," I told him.
And it was.

I said good night to my father, kissed
my sister, and went back to my room. I'll
miss my West Coast room and my house. But
I'm beginning to think about my other room
— the one on the East Coast. I like that
room too.

And I have a mother in Stoneybrook. I

realize I've missed her a lot lately. It'll be so wonderful to wake up in the morning and know my mother is in the same house. I also remember that I have good friends in Stoneybrook. And another sister. And a stepfather whom I've come to like a lot. We have a great time together.

I'm starting to look forward to tomorrow and the next day and the day after that. It's summertime. Time for fun.

Everything will be here when I come back.

Maybe in the fall Maggie and I can become better friends. I'll try even harder to understand her. I also want to become better friends with Amalia and Ducky.

The hardest person to leave is Sunny. I can see her house from my window. I remember the summer we'd sit near our windows and talk with walkie-talkies. That seems so long ago.

Where is that Sunny? Where is our old friendship?

Have I changed too?

I feel an ache in my heart whenever I think of Sunny. We didn't outgrow one another, the way you do some friends and certain childhood things like your training wheels, or certain clothes, or playing with dolls. I didn't outgrow Sunny, I lost her and I shouldn't have. Something went terribly wrong with our friendship. And it should not have happe

I thought I just saw Sunny at her window. I waved. I waited to see if the curtains would part and her window fly open. I held my breath. Maybe this was it. Maybe I'd go over to her house and we'd talk through the night until it was time for my flight tomorrow. Maybe she'd even ride out to the airport with me. Please, Sunny, I thought. Please wave back.

I waved again. Nothing.

Maybe she wasn't even there.

I could telephone her. And say what? "Good-bye." And then what?

Why doesn't Sunny call me? She knows I'm going away tomorrow.

Maybe one night of talking isn't enough to fix what has gone wrong between us.

For the first time in my life I'm going away without saying good-bye to Sunny. I wish with all my heart it wasn't so.

But it is.

Ann M. Martin

About the Author

ANN MATTHEWS MARTIN was born on August 12, 1955. She grew up in Princeton, NJ, with her parents and her younger sister, Jane.

Although Ann used to be a teacher and then an editor of children's books, she's now a full-time writer. She gets the ideas for her books from many different places. Some are based on personal experiences. Others are based on childhood memories and feelings. Many are written about contemporary problems or events.

All of Ann's characters are made up. But some of her characters are based on real people. Sometimes Ann names her characters after people she knows, other times she chooses names she likes.

In addition to California Diaries, Ann Martin has written many other books, including the Baby-sitters Club series. She has written twelve novels for young people, including *Missing Since Monday, With You or Without You, Slam Book,* and *Just a Summer Romance.*

Ann M. Martin does not live in California, though she does visit frequently. She lives in New York with her cats, Gussie, Woody, and Willy. Her hobbies are reading, sewing, and needlework — especially making clothes for children.

Look for #8

Maggie, Diary Two

2:30 P.M. Monday 7/13

Breakfast: Small bowl of cornflakes w/skim
milk, black coffee (no sugar)
Lunch: 1/2 tuna sandwich (NO mayo)/diet
soda/one apple (small)
Goal: Don't eat between meals.
Weight: 103 1/2 lbs.
Goal: 90 lbs.

    Starting today I, Maggie Blume, vow to
write down every bite that goes into my
mouth.
    I have to face facts. I am one of those
people who gain weight if they eat five

peanuts. I'll have to watch what I eat for the rest of my life. I might as well start now.

Everyone tells me I don't need to lose weight. They say I have a great body. They are WRONG WRONG WRONG. They don't see me when I'm in my underwear. They don't see me when I'm on the scale. They think I'm thin, but I'm FAT. Thirteen pounds. That's all I need.